FINISHING LINE PRESS

www.finishinglinepress.com

CIRCLING TOWARD HOME
Grassroots Baseball Prose, Meditations, and Images

prose and photography by

Bill Meissner

Finishing Line Press
Georgetown, Kentucky

CIRCLING TOWARD HOME

Grassroots Baseball Prose, Meditations, and Images

Publisher: Leah Huete de Maines
Editor: Christen Kincaid
Cover Art: Photo by Bill Meissner
Author Photo: Christine Meissner
Cover Design: Nathan Meissner

Order online: www.finishinglinepress.com
also available on amazon.com

Author inquiries and mail orders:
Finishing Line Press
P. O. Box 1626
Georgetown, Kentucky 40324
U. S. A.

Table of Contents

This book is dedicated, with love, to my wife, Christine, and our son, Nathan—always the greatest teammates, before, during, and after the game.

AUTHOR'S INTRODUCTION

If you look at a well-used baseball, you'll see that the scrapes and scuff marks resemble a map. I've followed that map for years, and during that time, the game of baseball has taken me on a kind of journey. Not a road trip, like the one you might take with a car or bicycle, following the winding back roads of America, but a journey just the same. It's led me through years and decades from childhood to adulthood, through stages of life where baseball meant everything to me, and other times when I fell away and completely forgot about it. What I eventually discovered is that baseball is a game which, in many ways, parallels human nature, with its aspirations and shortcomings, its disappointments and triumphs. The prose pieces, vignettes, and meditations in this book attempt to capture the essence of those moments.

The passages will introduce you to a wide variety of characters. The fields and grandstands are populated not only with pitchers and outfielders and groundskeepers, but with fathers and sons, girlfriends and wives, lovers and friends. You'll meet players who range in age from optimistic kids just learning the game to junior high kids dreaming of the Majors to 102-year-old veterans fondly gazing back on their careers. You'll also have glimpses of the players and fans who frequent the remote fields of the Yucatan in Mexico, Puerto Rico, and the Caribbean island of St. Thomas.

The ballfields themselves have their say, too, and if you take the time to listen, you'll hear the sometimes profound and wise, sometimes whimsical voices of the backstop, the scoreboard, outfield fences, line drives, and even the swirling clouds that gaze down on the game.

Several years ago, I began taking photos of abandoned, rural, or out-of-the-way amateur ball fields. They seemed to call out to me to honor them, to capture their spirit, the essence of their rustic beauty and character, and so I did. Of the thousands of photos I've taken, I've included my favorites in this collection.

Consider this thought, expressed by a coach, who might have doubled as a Zen master: A field is just a field. It's just an ordinary expanse with weeds and overgrown grass swirled into waves by the wind. It's no baseball field until you mark off the fair and foul lines with a wide reach of your arms. It's no diamond until you mark home by where your feet finally choose to stand.

From there, you play the game. No matter who you are, or what size, or how strong, all you really need to do is catch a ball, or meet the ball with a bat, and then, maybe, to tell a good story afterward.

Yes, a worn baseball is a map. But only if you look at it closely enough. Only if you dream. So, begin the journey with me. Take a step toward home plate. It's always closer than you think.

PART ONE

Dancing Onto the Field

THE HEART OF THE BASEBALL

A baseball has a soul. This I know to be true.

Maybe it's not exactly the kind of soul most people picture. But beneath its leather shell and those 369 yards and 941 feet of wool and yarn and string, it's still a soul. The soul of the man or woman in a remote mountain town in Costa Rica who hand-sewed the 108 stitches on the cover, the ball propped and motionless on a wooden stand. The soul of the person who lifts it from a field and throws it, the person who catches it in a mitt, the person who keeps dropping it to the hard ground. The soul of someone who hits it with a bat and sends it five feet, or fifty, or five hundred. The soul of the person doesn't believe in themselves yet—who thinks they're too small, or too weak, or too different. Someone who swings at it, missing it again and again, then keeps swinging until they finally make contact.

These things I believe—a baseball has a soul, and it's a lot like the spirit of the person who stands on an emerald sea of grass that is deep, but still solid and rippling. As they cradle the leather sphere and make a wish, they look toward home and think about where they've been, and where they're going, and where they are right now.

Right now, lift the ball from its slumber inside an old leather glove. Run your fingertips along the worn smile of its red stitches and sense the dreams, circled inside its cushioned core. Feel its weight—heavy and light as the whole earth. Feel the way a baseball is round, but not perfect, the way it nestles in the palm of your hand the same way it might fit into the bowl of a bird's nest.

Feel its vibrations, its steady heartbeat. Though it seems to be silent, listen for that faint humming sound, a melody coming from deep down. Don't be afraid to let yourself sing along. Or dance. Or believe that you, too, could rise suddenly into the air and fly.

TAKE A WALK AROUND THIS ABANDONED BASEBALL FIELD: A ROMANCE

Though the backstop of this ragged field is curved and bent and dented, the wires still braid together in diamond shapes, like lovers who refuse to let go.

First base is a piece of plywood someone tossed down. It's only an inch thick, but has buoyed up the soles of a thousand cleats or tennis shoes. Safe, or out: those are the only two words the first base knows.

Second base is tentative, its wood warped, curled slightly by the staring sun. Wan and bleached, with a dark spiral knot in its center, it worries perpetually about its heart being stolen.

Third base whimpers. Because triples are rare, this lid from a cardboard box always feels ignored, lonely, and not touched often enough. Like the floor of a house where people rarely come to visit, it's always waiting.

The first and third base lines are mute, and undecided. If you stand at home plate and look their way, there's no chalk line to tell you whether a ball is fair or foul. You just have to know by sight, by memory, by intuition. Gaze down the line, as a twisting fly ball drops from the sky, and—like an honest umpire—try to make the correct call.

The pitcher's mound is a misnomer. Here, it's not a mound at all, but a circle of flattened grass. Still, when the pitcher draws his or her arm back to throw the ball, the earth seems to rise, to arch its back. It becomes the focal point, the center of the diamond, the place where the game begins, the place from which light sparkles.

The grass of the outfield is always overgrown. Always. But get used to it. It can never be tamed, can never be separated from the wild weeds or stark saplings that spike from it, their stalks scratching the morning sky. The grass has learned to fight inertia, to slow a rolling baseball, to arch and bow like breaking ocean waves, to spin itself into whirlpools, to curl into a cave for ants and beetles, a diving board for locusts that flick and spring. On hot afternoons, you can hear the sound of unseen insects clicking and buzzing. And, on still spring evenings, when the insects go silent, if you listen hard enough, you can hear the sound of the grass growing: a soft sighing song.

There are no outfield walls, of course. The field goes on forever. Forever. Forever.

The gusting wind is the owner of this field, and patrols it constantly. If the wind is calm everywhere else on earth, it will be gusting on this one small field. The wind's mission in life is to ripple your T-shirt, blow your hair into your eyes, to flip your ball cap from your head and send it cart-wheeling across the infield, making you feel foolish and small. Its mission is to rush across the infield, to summon the field's spirits from the patches of dry, bare soil, to raise them and show them to you in whirling dust devils.

The wind can knock down the pride of any line drive. Or, if it decides to, the wind can push a ball—hit high into the outfield—farther than it ever imagined it could go.

The batter's box is not a box; it knows no corners. It's more of an oval, carved into the soil by the thousands of batters stepping into hundreds of thousands of pitches. After years of use, it has taken on the shape of an eye, as if it's looking deep into the earth.

And last but not least, the plate. What about home plate?

There is no thick, anchored black and white rubber slab here, like the ones on regulation fields. In fact, there's nothing here at all, except a worn spot, so you have to imagine home. Or you could try to duplicate it, using whatever you can find: a flattened leather mitt, a book, a left-behind tennis shoe, a discarded high school love note held flat by four small stones. Maybe even a square of sunlight. Or a slice of a dream.

Home plate: It's the place where, after the game is over, you meet at midnight, one on each side, with your new lover. It's the place where the moonlight shines down and makes the powdery dust between you glisten at the moment you lean toward each other for that first kiss.

CHALK LINES

The spring of freshman year, when the ball field at the edge of town exploded with grass brighter and greener than I'd ever seen it before, I played baseball. My best friend Steve Lyon and I practiced on the old West School Field; all afternoon, we'd pitch and hit and field in the heat, until, around five o'clock, we'd cross the highway intersection to Kluge's gas station, sit on card table chairs, and drink cold strawberry sodas.

Sometimes we'd take off our ball caps and gaze at them, noticing where the sweat had evaporated from the bills in salty rings: pools of sweat, lakes of sweat, oceans of sweet sweat. Our t-shirts stuck to metal chairs as, winded, we'd lean forward and stare at the dank, paint-chipped wall. Without saying a word, we knew what each other was thinking: though we were only thirteen, we were imagining chalk lines all the way to the Majors.

We already knew the Major Leaguer's yearning. It's that squint when there's no sun in the eyes. It's the eagerness for home runs, for diving catches, even though you're nothing more than a gawky kid, even though sometimes you feel lost, walking beneath an endless sky of splintered high school bleachers and rusting beams.

FOR THOSE WHO CHOOSE TO HIT INTO THE WIND

Lifting a worn baseball, he stands on this rutted field, closing his eyes, focusing. At age thirty, he hasn't hit a ball for years, but hopes he can find that skill again. Optimism is the key, he thinks. He has to believe in himself. It doesn't matter that it feels like the wind has been blowing hard toward him for the past few years.

He opens his eyes, tosses the ball in front of his face, sees its slow rotation, like the earth in space, then swings hard.

He misses, the ball thuds to the sod, and he lets out a short laugh.

He picks the ball up, swings, and misses again. He shakes his head, wondering how he has lost his knack for this. Ten years ago, on the town team, he could hit any curve or fastball the pitchers threw to him.

He picks up the ball for a third attempt. The wind subsides, diminishing to a light breeze that falls to its knees. Calmness becomes a sensation in itself, caressing the bare skin of his arms. He tosses the ball in front of his face, and this time he brings the bat around to the ball instinctively—not a planned or practiced swing, but powerful and quick, smooth and seamless as the bat parts the air suddenly. His muscles wake from their long sleep, and the bat finds the ball in its center, that exact spot where wood falls in love with leather. A solid vibration resonates through the grains of the bat, into his hands, up through his wrists and arms and all the way to his heart.

In that instant, the old feeling comes back to him: a feeling rising from deep inside, one that's been lost for a long time. The ball climbs high, higher, tracing a towering arc in the curve of blue. It lands deep in left center, takes two quick bounces between the pine trees, rolls, and finally comes to rest.

He's a little surprised by how far it carries.

THE EX-BASEBALL STAR STEPS OUT OF
RETIREMENT

Stepping onto the field again, he cracks a few fly balls, the bat in his hands remembering those solid hits, those homers the crowd confused with distant white birds.

The older you get, he thinks, the more you notice the chalk lines—chalk lines on the grass, on your face. The memories flicker past like baseball cards in the spokes of a bicycle.

He lopes to the outfield. Trying to make a perfect throw from left to second is like aiming a frayed shoelace through a rusted eyelet.

As he jogs across the third base line and into the dugout, dust wheezes in the hourglass of his throat. He'll head home, sip a lite beer in the back yard, the ball game blaring from the scratchy speakers of the radio. His lips lift into a smile as he watches his son and daughter play catch by the fence, the sound of the cheering fans rising, then falling, then rising again.

TODAY'S FORECAST

1. Clouds

We are called cirrus, cumulus, stratus, nimbus. We are the gods of the sky. The batting cage foolishly thinks it can hold us inside it. Summer afternoons, we rule the field, causing a new baseball, popped high in the air, to be lost in our whiteness. Other days, we cover the sky with a tarpaulin of gray, and everyone down there feels suddenly melancholy.

But most times, we grace the field with beauty, painting the azure sky with our wispy artwork. People look for ancient faces, hidden in our swirls. Though we know we'll always be pushed away by the wind, we try to stall, and linger over a field, waiting for a high fly ball to almost—but never quite—touch us.

Our wings grow wings.
Like dreams, we always seem so close, yet so far away.

2. Thunder

I am the anti-god of baseball games. Though some may try, there is no arguing with me. I always repeat the same warning with my deep, guttural words: *Leave*, I command. *Don't play today. Play tomorrow. Play tomorrow.*

3. Rain

The players claim the field is theirs. The loyal hometown fans say the same thing.

But they are all wrong.

I am a rainstorm, and I—along with my companion the lightning—own the field.

Just watch: The moment I decide to start my sudden downpour, players duck into the dugout, fans in the stands scatter, run to their cars, and roll up their windows. Then they sit there, helpless, as I write my name across their dusty windshields.

4. Sunlight

Some days, when the sky seems darkest and most overcast, I surprise you by tossing a bright yellow wedge of myself on the far side of the field. Then I slide it right toward you, brightening your face at the same time I illuminate the grass's green dreams beneath your feet.

AMATEUR BASEBALL TEAM NAMES THAT ROLL OFF THE TONGUE: SAY THEM PROUDLY, AND AS FAST AS YOU CAN

Rockies. Red Birds. Red Devils. Blue Ox. Rox. Flames. Comets. Chargers. Chuckers. Stingers. Shockers. Bombers. Bandits. Orphans. Gnats. Gussies. Kernels. Wood Ducks. Lakes. Lakers. Springers. Muskies. Loons. Swans. Catch 'n Release. Steves. Skis. Spiders. Serpents. Saints. Villains. Diamondbacks. Dutchmen. Icemen. Freeze. Jacks. Lumberjacks. Aces. Bucs. Bees. Fusion. Wildcats. Polecats. Hogs. Hawks. Stone Poneys. Roadrunners. Bullfrogs. River Dogs. River Cats. Rail Dogs. Mudcats. Mudhens. Snurdbirds. LoGators. Billy Goats. Buttermakers.

THIRTEEN MEDITATIONS ON THE SOUND OF THE BAT

Listen: The sound of a wooden bat hitting a baseball is so sharp and resonant that if you close your eyes, you can almost see it, like a flash of light.

The bat hitting the ball is not like the soft, gentle sound of an egg cracking. It's the sound you hear when lightning parts the air for a split second, and the sky claps its hands.

It surprises the sleeping air around home plate, wakes the grass blades of a whole sandlot field, startles an entire stadium.

It's the jolting alarm that sets everything into motion: fielders, ump, base runners. Like the starting gun at a race, it signals the batter to sprint down the first base line; it lifts fans and onlookers to their feet.

It's sudden, like the wings of a startled thrush as it bursts from a branch. It's been said that a sightless person, sitting behind home plate, can tell whether a hit is a foul or a ground ball or a solid home run simply by the pitch and intensity of the bat hitting the ball.

It's the explosion of polished wood striking fast-pitched leather.

It's a sound you feel as much as hear, a sound that echoes deep in your chest. When a batter swings and the bat shatters, it's not the same. It's a sad, splintering sound, like a bone breaking, or a dead tree limb falling to the hard ground.

But the solid hit—oh, the solid hit: the batter feels its vibration in his hands and wrists and forearms and all the way down to his roots.

The crack of the bat: Baseball's punctuation. Its music. Its shot that, sometimes, is heard around the world.

It's the first note of a song.

Listen: It's sound of an eye, closed and blind for a long time, finally opening to see the world.

It's when all time begins and ends. If Albert Einstein were in the stands with a group of fans, he'd hear the sound of the bat and calculate energy and distance. He'd tell you exactly how long it would take a long home run—if it kept on flying—to reach the stars.

THE BACKSTOP

Like a nurturing grandparent, it's always there, standing behind you, its hopes for your future rising like wings. Its wires might be bent in places, or corroded, but never broken. A pitch that skips beyond the catcher's mitt, an errant throw from shortstop or right field to home—the backstop brings them all to an abrupt halt. It's there—solid, stalwart, and always willing to make your errors look a little less like mistakes.

THE THIRD BASE LINE FOUL POLE EXPRESSES A VERY IMPORTANT OPINION

I am always fair. So I only ask you one thing: Don't ever call me the fowl pole.

PITCH BY PITCH

The game begins with him, as he adjusts his cap, tugs at his jersey, leans forward, peers in for the sign, nods.

He's learned to take his pitches one at a time, to not think about the next ninety or one-hundred he'll throw during the game. He can't lose his focus. One, two, three strikes, and a batter's out. Don't think about what might happen, or what could go wrong. Pitch by pitch—that's how he lives his life.

When he's at home, or out with his girlfriend or the guys, he might relax, and laugh, and say nothing matters. But on the mound, things do. Strike, ball: These are the only two words that matter. When he steps to the mound, he's a tightrope walker, balancing, pawing the dirt with his toe as if it were that easy to level the earth.

One, two, three. It all seems so simple.

Right now he lifts the ball from his glove, cradles it, gives it time to memorize his fingerprints. He swings into the slow, elaborate dance of his wind-up, then reaches all the way back as if he could touch the horizon. He pauses a moment, the ball, his life, his whole future balancing back there in the palm of his hand.

He knows that, on any one throw, he could fail. He might see the bat whip around, sending his best pitch flying a mile. He might slip slightly on the mound and fall off balance, the ball veering far from where it was aimed. Might see his coach, about to take him out of the game, his eyes fixed to the ground as he saunters from the dugout.

Still, he throws this one as hard as he can. It's the most he can do—to strive for just one perfect pitch in an imperfect world. One pitch that leaves his fingertips and turns to a streak of light cutting through all that darkness.

THE ARC

The father and son play catch in the back yard until late afternoon. He loves to watch his son catch the looping throws, loves to see him throw the ball back, the baseball rising in an arc from the low shadows of the trees and igniting in the sunlight before it falls back to shadowy earth.

He listens to the rhythmic beat of the ball in their leather pockets. You could keep time by a game of catch, this steady beat, this throwing back and forth, back and forth, each swing of the arm like the sweep of a pendulum, each throw another year.

After an off-target throw, the ball skips past the son's glove and rolls to the back corner of the yard.

"My fault," the father calls.

"No, my fault," the boy echoes, running to retrieve the ball.

It's the language of ballplayers. Without saying any more, they each know what the other means: no one is to blame. There is no right or wrong in a game of catch on a sandlot, no winners or losers. If you drop a ball, you just pick it up again. If you toss it off target, maybe you'll throw straight to the pocket the next time. It's a humble language, and a language of belief.

It's a game where the spinning ball ties the horizons to each other as the sunset begins to paint the sky a brilliant red. It's a line drawn from palm to palm, connecting one generation to the next, and the next.

It's a simple game of catch. And it's so much more.

THE NIGHT GAME

Though I'm never quite as bright, I imitate the sun after it slides below the lip of the earth. A towering fly ball, hit above the view of my unblinking eyes, turns to shadows for a moment, but it always comes back to the light.

They always come back to me, their shepherd of brightness.

I illuminate the two-hop ground ball, the line drive that's coming at you fast. I protect you, save you. I attach shadows to the feet of the players, making them feel like they never walk alone on the broad field.

Late in the evening, in the ninth inning, I light up the eggshell faces of the fans in the stands as they tip their faces toward me in anticipation of the final out.

As they leave the grandstands, before I grow dim and finally close my eyes, I watch the fans slowly filter out. Soon they'll drive through that dark valley toward their homes. I hope that, as they do, the insides of the skulls will glow faintly with the memory of me. And that, somehow, I will still light their way.

IF HITS COULD SPEAK

The Line Drive

I always draw a straight arrow toward my destination. I never waver or have any doubts. Even though I know I might be caught, I believe in myself.

I come flying at you faster than you expected. I am truth. Watch out for me. I may surprise you.

The Fly Ball

I rise from home and trace a magnificent arc. I'm so far above you that I should have a crown on my head. You never know how far I will carry, or where the wind might take me. But the point is, when I rise, those fans who have been sitting in the stands with their heads bowed for so long will suddenly tip their faces hopefully toward the sky and admire me.

The Foul Tip

I arrive unexpectedly, in a split second, before you can move. If you are a catcher, an umpire, or a player warming up in the on-deck circle, beware. I break fingers, wrists, ribs, jaws. I'll knock the wind out of you and stop you, suddenly, from talking.

I'm fast as death, fast as life, and you have no time to react.

Like the screen behind home plate, I'll make you sting, and sing with pain.

The Ground Ball

Hear what I have to say: They call me humble, since I bow down to everything else on the field. Sometimes I roll no further than ten or fifteen feet. I'm always ignored, underrated. Some people laugh at me. They call me weak, a dribbler, a worm-burner.

But do not underestimate my potential. Unlike the long fly ball that always boasts about its height and shows off in the sky, I can roll, steadily, beyond the reach of a shortstop's glove and win a game.

You may not believe me. But by the time I've told you this, I've just rolled right past you.

THINGS ARE ALWAYS SO CLOSE

For an umpire, there can be no hesitations. It's always a hundredth of a second that matters. The right foot of a batter just an inch from the bag at first base, a ball snapping in a glove, a tag on the ankle of a runner sliding into second or third.

Things are always so close.

After twenty-some years behind the plate, Harold Brace knows an umpire has to be focused, accurate. You have to lean forward and concentrate on the game. No time for—like the players in the dugout—gazing off at some swirling cloud patterns. No time for casually tossing a handful of sunflower seeds into your mouth. You just bend forward with that thick black mask and chest protector, bend forward for so long you begin to feel like a crouched crustacean.

His existence is steady, consistent. Things start and end with him. Whenever he decides, he can make time speed forward, calling *Play ball!* or stop time from moving.

Still, he realizes that no one likes an umpire, so they're forever alone on the field. Between innings, the players talk and laugh, give each other high fives, but no one talks to the ump as he lingers there, a few feet from the batter's box. Sometimes he pulls off his protective mask and turns to stare into the bleachers, as if he hopes that he'll recognize someone he knows up there. And maybe they'll nod to him. Or maybe they won't.

In life, and in baseball, he knows he has to make the right call. There are sharp lines drawn between everything. Black and white. You have to know fair from foul, strike from ball, safe from out, and nothing in between. You have to have faith in yourself.

It's a privilege, and a burden at the same time, weighing down his shoulders.

But then, sometimes the doubts begin to creep in. *What about the gnawing feelings that you've made the wrong call?* he wonders. *What if you're at fault, on a close play, for turning someone's win into a loss? What if you're responsible for smothering someone's dreams, or breaking a heart?* Those are the questions that, like fastballs bouncing off his chest protector, knock the wind out of him.

THE GRASSHOPPER KING

The instant it stops rolling, he claims it, and now it's his little domain. He owns it—every inch, every country on this small empire. He clings to it, exploring its map of red stitches, its well-traveled leather terrain that keeps invading his lush forest of green.

Owns it, until, finally, tiring of this kingdom, he decides to spring from it with a sudden click, flicker through the air with a soft buzz, then disappear in the deep weeds beyond the third base line, where he waits to conquer the next small world that rolls toward him.

THE SCOREBOARD

One thing about it: it never lies. Your hits, your errors appear, inning by inning, in the white boxes. Like an all-knowing god, it keeps track of you, following your every move, and there's no hiding from it in the dugout.

Your totals, your final scores are always there, in plain sight, for all the world to see.

PREGAME RITUAL: A STILL LIFE

They arrive much earlier than they need to, pulling into the parking lot in pickup trucks and beat-up cars, clouds of dust spiraling behind bumpers. Hopping out, they filter toward the outfield fence—their appointed gathering spot—and take a seat on the grass. From there, they gaze longingly through a section of the fence, a doorway that opens to the bright, Eden-like garden, the place they'll jog onto in an hour. But they don't talk about baseball. Not yet. For now, between sips of spring water, they chat and joke about summer jobs, girlfriends, car repair, hassles with their old man.

Then they suddenly go silent. During that pause, one of them bends closer to the fence, lifts his hands, curls his fingers into the diamonds as if to hold it still. Another one leans back, ready to tuck his glove under his head like a pillow, as if he's about to dream.

THE HIT HEARD ACROSS THE COUNTRY

At this small-town field, there is no outfield fence, just a slanted bank of grass that leads to County Highway 8. On a long fly ball to left during the Region 11C championship game, the visiting outfielder races back, back, back, then gives up as the berm rises beneath his cleats. The sound of that home run ball, slapping the concrete, carries all the way to the cheering hometown fans.

The ball bounces once, twice, then right into the flatbed of a pickup truck passing on the highway. Three fans wearing feed caps—who clutch cans of Hamms and work at the implement company—laugh and joke about the ball rolling around in that flatbed as the truck parades down the main streets of the rival towns of Clear Lake or Luxemburg or Farming or Eden Valley.

After another beer, one of them gestures, describing how the ball could ride the flatbed past those towns, from county highway to county highway, to the state line, even, and then all the way across the U.S.A.

You bet, he thinks. It could happen. It sure as heck could happen.

PART TWO

Love and Baseball

THE BASEBALL LOVER

So far, it's a no hitter. She's still on the couch, staring at Dateline, and he's in the corner, oiling his glove with his tongue. This is the tension of extra innings—all day he's waited on deck, counting the circles chalked on his brain.

She claims he wears his yellow baseball cap too much. Sometimes he even sleeps with it on his face like an egg yolk, while her breathing makes the sound of wind through empty bleachers. All night dreams flow from his cap's brim: He's sliding toward home plate, and the slide never stops—through the dugout, under the grandstand, across the sandlot, into the skin of his childhood, the seat of his pants burning like birth.

At the commercial, he switches on the baseball game. Someone is trying to steal home—his legs are the wings of anxious birds. He will never move in slow motion, not even in the replay.

Here comes the pitch, here comes the runner. He slides next to her on the couch, begins whispering sweet baseball scores into her ear.

INSTRUCTION MANUAL:
SOME BASIC SKILLS, AND ONE OR TWO EXTRAS

1) The Hit.

You don't have to see it fly. After you swing, you don't have to watch it climb in the air, cutting the blue dome of sky in half. You know, by the resonant vibrations in the bat that it's not too far down the handle, nor is it so far out on the barrel that it feels dull and tentative. You could even have your eyes closed. You know the ball is up there, spinning into the splintering sunlight. You know by the feel of the wood in your hands—a connection that doesn't sting your palms—that you've hit it well.

It's the intuition of a ball player. It's the same way he or she looks into someone's eyes for the first time and knows they're a friend, or a lover, or even a future spouse.

It's the knowing, after years of practice and trial and error. And error. It's the moment of beauty, the instant of—after being lost for a long time—finding something and knowing that it's right. Not just that it's good—but that it's extraordinary, and it means something.

It's hitting the baseball on a small, sweet spot—the size of a dime—on the barrel. It's not even having to squint to find it in the sky. Instead, you lean into a trot, knowing that the ball will go deep, that it will arc and arc and arc until it finds its way over the fence.

2) The Pitch.

Rear back as far as you can, as if you're touching the distant horizon behind you and gathering some strength from it. Then snap the ball forward. The ball must trace the exact line that you've imagined in your head. Sometimes it's a straight line, and other times it involves a sharp curve between your release and its destination. The ball must spin in the air like a planet, lost in space, hungry to return home. It must go quickly: no doubt about it—no lagging, no waiting, no falling asleep somewhere halfway between. It must cut through the still, humid air like a meteor burns through the thick atmosphere. It must make the batter blink as it strikes the catcher's mitt with a small thudding explosion of dust and he hears the umpire call out Steee-rike!

But there's more: It must be as real and intense the connection between you and your lover the first time you glance, with passion, into each other's eyes: quick, decisive, instantaneous, and precisely aimed. Precisely aimed.

Now: Pick up the ball. Rotate it in your hand, getting to know its smooth spots, the tiny ridges of its stitches. Then reach back and throw it as hard and fast as you can, and watch it spin toward home: so red and white and red and white and blinding.

3) *The Catch.*

They say a great left fielder knows where the ball will be hit before the batter swings, but that's not true. It's not that easy. There's a lot more to it: You have to wait, wait that split second as it rises from the bat. You have to judge the power of the hit, the trajectory, the height that it might fly. At that moment, your brain is like a precise scientist's, instantly calculating apogee and perigee, angles and timing.

Then all those thoughts vanish from your mind and, bowing your head briefly, you dig in with your cleats, pushing off the world like a runner who plans to sprint all the way around it. That's when you cut a diagonal across the outfield, dashing toward that one spot, hoping to reach it before the ball does. As you run, your pulse beats hard in your heels, your leg muscles go taut and burn like wires. You know you have only five or six seconds to save the ball from scraping its smooth pale skin on the ground.

As the ball falls from the vacuum of the sky, you wait until the last instant and then jump, reaching upward as if you could catch the moon, your glove opening like a hungry mouth.

Time slows down during the leap.

When you're at your highest point, the fans who watch from the stands believe that you'll never come down, that you might actually be able to fly.

That's when you catch your lover's face in your hands and pull them close, close, close to you. Even when the hard, indifferent earth lifts its broad shoulders and crashes into you, you don't let go.

NOTE LEFT FOR THE WIDOWS OF THE OVER-THIRTY BASEBALL PLAYERS

For you, who wake at seven-thirty some morning and find me gone, my duffel bag missing from the closet, a note scrawled on a smudged scorecard on the clean couch, my spilled flakes of Wheaties cemented to the kitchen table like some strange hieroglyphs…

For you, who must endure the creaking of my arching muscles as I sleep, the odors of high school T-shirts with moth holes, of muddied spikes that curl into themselves in the corner of the entryway, of musty, waterlogged memories that roll across the floor each evening…

For you, who never question the logic of my lopsided brain, and why I insist on healing broken and rebroken bats again and again with glue, wood screws, miles of masking tape, and hope…

For you, who, when I lean toward the doorway, glove in hand, asking if it's okay to play some ball, shape your smooth pink lips around the word *Go*.

This note is for you.

Forgive me, your husband, lost somewhere in the bleachers thirty years deep, searching for that one child who looks like me.

This note is for you. Listen to the most honest thing I could say, the resonant sound of my best hit: I love you.

I want you to always remember that it's a kind of love that makes me leave to play this game each day, that makes me run those bases under a huge, indifferent sky.

And it's love that pulls me back to the house hours later, winded but a little younger each time, to stand as close to you as humanly possible, to gaze into the clear roundness of your eyes that don't care if I've won or lost.

WHEN SHE PITCHES

When she pitches, she lifts me from her glove, her fingertips caressing my seams gently but firmly. She gazes at me fondly, as if she's memorizing the scars beneath my stitches, or else is about to sing to me.

She goes into her wind up, and it's as though we're doing a graceful, underwater ballet. Then she reaches back, tendons humming like the strings of a harp, and she holds me there for a second as though she's touching her past, though I know her future's coming soon. I never doubt her strength. Her arm swings forward, waking the air around me, until I feel like a small planet spinning out of orbit.

But I never lose my direction.

When she pitches, I become a kind of song, and like a swiftly migrating white bird, I always know the way home.

THE CLEANUP HITTER'S GIRLFRIEND

Watching him intently, she waits for him. She longs for him, and hopes he feels the same, but she can't tell him that, not right now. He's at bat, focusing on the pitcher's knuckles as he grips the ball.

She saves a place for him next to her at the edge of the picnic table. The umbrella she holds will protect her, she believes, from whatever is about to come her way—the too-bright sun, the gray and the rain, or something in between.

To her, the game seems long; it seems to last for days, weeks. She waits for him to step out of that batter's box, to finally cross the chalk line that seems to hold him in, then walk toward her, reach his fingers through the fence, and gently touch her hand.

HOW MUCH SHE KNOWS

She knows him: every stitch, every seam, every scuff mark on his tough cover. Sometimes his stitches smile, and sometimes they frown. And she knows the inside, when that cover is suddenly loosened: the layers of gray and blue strings coiled around and around into a crazy cortex of memories. A cortex that feels joy, and sometimes, from all that spinning, a headachy dizziness, a lostness. She knows there's pain in there, too, held deep inside the core by tight winding.

Most of all, she knows what he'll say before he even says it. "Love," he says, and she knows he means it, and she echoes the word back to him.

ZEN AND THE ART OF OUTFIELDING

First Inning.

What I like most is the room to move, the room to flow under the high flies, waiting for their whiteness to cover my palm. There's a beauty in the outfield, a grace. Out here, on the green sea, no one touches me. But it's a lonely place, too, and sometimes I feel like the last human being on earth. I toss long throws to second or home, my only lines of connection. No one seems to know what I feel, to love it as much as I do.

As I stand there, waiting for the game's first pitch, I hear a voice in my head—it's the voice of the woman I love. *Look out into the world*, she said to me this morning.

Second Inning.

This morning, in our apartment, we sat at a small wood table in the green kitchen, my glove placed next to my bowl of cereal. I'd been talking baseball all during breakfast. The standings. Today's starting pitchers. The championship game coming up this afternoon. During a pause, she took a sip of orange juice, then looked up at me and said: *Just don't let it be everything to you. Sometimes you have to look beyond yourself, your game.* At first, I gave her my patented shrug, and a puzzled expression, as if I didn't know what she meant. But if she didn't say things like that, I would never feel the way I do about her.

Third Inning.

An outfielder has a certain liking for fences, walls. Sometimes they outline my life. I'll tell you that walls seem to contain you better than open fields do. They stop those line drives between center and left that skip by too quickly for any human to reach. They send the ball careening toward me, so I can barehand it and nail the runner trying to stretch it to third. You might say that an outfielder is a little in love with walls. They speak strongly to my shoulders when I back into them; they let me know my limitations.

Sometimes the true test is holding onto the ball you've just caught, even though you've run full speed into the wall and everything hurts.

Yes, the fences make the game.

Fourth Inning.

Fans, she says to me. *The fans are only superficial. They don't know you the way I know you.*

I know what she says is true. I realize the fans love me, in their way. And I appreciate them. Sometimes the sound of their cheers is like pure sunlight in my ears. But the fans admire me only in my little world, surrounded by lines and fences. They only admire me in my white pinstriped uniform that glows beneath the center field floodlights; they don't see my shadow. They don't see me, sitting at the breakfast table in the green kitchen, clumsily lifting my cup of coffee, spilling some of the brown liquid on the table. They don't see the real me, dropping my peanut butter toast to the floor in the dim light of morning.

I do, she says to me, and she rounds her lips beautifully to say the words. When she does, I don't reply; I just brush her hair back with my glove hand, touch her cheek with my bare hand.

Fifth Inning.

A high fly to deep center excites me more than an easy pop-up that takes just a step or two to catch. If a ball is hit right at me, there's no challenge to it. I like the hits I need to run for. I like gliding to my right or my left to the place where I know the ball will land. Then I wait—almost casually—for the ball to finally drop out of orbit, surprised, as my leather glove closes solidly around it.

Sixth Inning.

A game isn't a game unless it's a close game, I think. Sometimes, when I'm standing out there, toeing the grass, watching batter after batter strike out or ground out, I think Let them get another run or two. Let them start some small fires.

What good is playing if it's not hit for hit, run for run? I wonder. What does winning mean if you always win by half a dozen? What good is winning if you never lose?

Closeness. Closeness is everything.

Seventh Inning.

Timing. It's what I think about during a game. It's knowing where you'll catch the ball even before the batter hits it. Timing is knowing when to dive for the line drive that's sinking fast, it's knowing which shoestring catches to go for, which are out of range.

If I drop a fly ball, I'm the only one to blame. Infielders can bobble a grounder, still throw the runner out. With an outfielder, it's decisive: the fly ball cannot touch the ground, or I die a little, right there in front of everyone.

I know that timing is everything when you're growing older. It's knowing the loss of a wasted moment, feeling the regret as you let it drop just beyond your fingertips.

As you back toward the wall, timing is understanding the moment, with its correct spring of leg muscles, its reach, its squeeze.
Thinking about it, ready for it. Yes.

Eighth Inning.
That one night, when she didn't come to my game, the outfield grass felt like crushed apples, crushed apples, crushed apples.

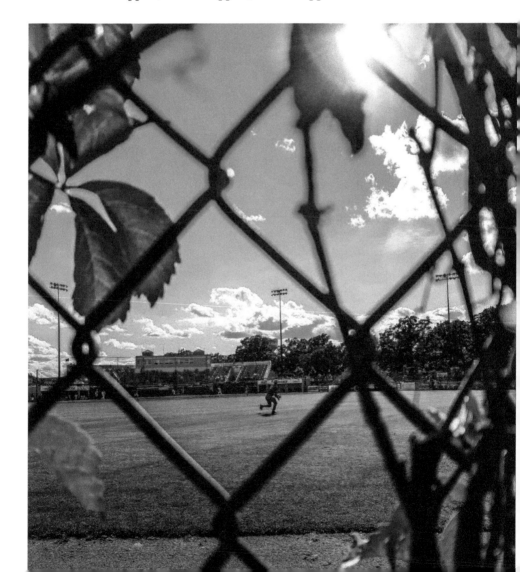

Ninth Inning.

The score is tied after nine innings. The opposing team's best power hitter swings, and the ball rises toward deep center. It's high and long and spinning with all its strength. I turn, race back at full speed, watching the ball over my shoulder all the while. At first, it feels like I'm running in slow motion, and the only sounds are the gasps of my breath, the hushing of my cleats in the short-cropped grass. The ball, a fleck of dust on the eye, begins its descent, and it appears it's going to clear the fence. *Uncatchable*, everyone in the stands thinks. Just out of reach.

The solid wall rushes toward my back, and know I have to time my leap.

I spring upward. Full extension, my left arm stretching until all my muscles scream. The glove opens hungrily, lovingly for the ball, and from this height, I think I my forehead can break through the heavy layer of the sky. The fans rise to their feet and scream for me, and I think I hear her voice calling for me, for the game, for the outfielder.

The next instant, I hit the wall hard, and to everyone's amazement, I hold on.

After the game, stepping through the exit gate, I look out into the world.

And there she is: at the far end of the gravel parking lot—the woman I love, leaning her hip against the door of her car. She's standing motionless, as if she's been waiting for me for years. Jogging toward her, I weave through the dull hulls of the parked cars, then pause in front of her. Her lips curve into a smile. I time it perfectly, sliding my arms around her, catching her. And at the same moment, she's catching me. And we hold on. We hold on. Yes, we hold on.

BASEBALL WIFE AT THE START OF THE SEASON

It's lovely to watch: she's never swung at a baseball before, but when her husband pitches to her, she swings and Monarch butterflies rise from the wooden barrel. She swings and sunlight scatters like shards of splintered glass. Rescued from the bottom of the duffel, his well-used batting gloves are loose on her slim hands, grime darkening the leather palms like storm clouds.

She swings again and the clouds vanish. Swings once more and a Canadian goose arcs gracefully over the field, returning north for the season.

Though he tells her to take a break, she won't step out of the batter's box. He realizes she'd stay on this diamond until evening, until it's too almost dark to see the ball, her hands learning the resonant song of leather and wood, wood and leather. She crouches like she's memorizing every scratched scar on that home plate, levels the bat over it like she's leveling the earth, nods at him to toss her the next pitch.

Later, in the middle of the night, the two of them lie on a wrinkled field of sheets. He knows he'd cross a thousand chalk lines for her. She reaches toward him, her soft, strong arms aching, but still dreaming of just one more swing that would hit the full moon squarely and shatter it to luminous pieces, doubling the stars in the night sky.

HOW MUCH YOU CAN SEE

Besides looking deeply into the eyes of the person you love, there's nothing more beautiful than a peaceful ballfield, in early spring, lit by the slanting late afternoon sunlight.

PART THREE

In the Other Leagues

THE DREAM KIDS

They're from Puerto Rico, Mexico, Venezuela, Dominican Republic, or some tiny Caribbean island you may never have heard about. They are the keepers of dreams, dreams that, though they start small, inflate and rise toward the sky.

Those dreams urge them to play ball, so each day on the cobblestone streets of villages and towns, in alleys, in narrow spaces between walls of concrete or adobe, they play. They play, filling, with laughter, whatever open space is given to them. They use sticks and rubber balls, or wood bats that are too big and heavy for them. They will swing, tirelessly, until they finally make contact. They play on sun-blistered, glass and can-littered, grassless lots where rocks—poking their foreheads through the soil—make the ball take sudden, uneven hops.

Still, the kids will climb any fence or wall to get there. They will run onto the diamond in frayed sandals, or bare feet, and catch the ball with gloves or their bare hands.

And, through their smiles, they will tell you their names, as if to say remember me.

Yes, they will dream. They will tell you that they love to play baseball, and someday, they will play in the Major Leagues. And as you listen, you realize you have no choice but to believe them.

LA TRIBUNA, PUERTO AVENTURAS, MEXICO

Simple as it is, this vintage grandstand has everything you will ever need: A view of the powdery infield, with an X to mark the field's hidden heart. A path leading across center field toward your casa in the village, in case you get lost. Pinol: some roasted corn starch, if you feel like a snack. A sky of corrugated tin, so that Chaak, the elusive rain god, won't drench you with a sudden downpour of warm tropical rain. Solid concrete, to protect you from a shuddering earthquake. A wire fence in front, to block any errant throws, or fluttering foul balls. Names of lovers scrawled on the side wall. Always the names of lovers.

SO THEY CAN BE HEARD:
SUNDAY AFTERNOON JUEGO DE BEISBOL IN COBA,
WITH MEGAPHONES

At the small field in the Maya village of Coba, Mexico, limestone rocks, from some forgotten ancient Maya ruin, decorate the ground around the stout grandstands. Chicken wire clings to poles hewn from trees. The poles are crooked and bent, but they still point upward to el sol, Kinich Ahau, the sun god. The chicken wire stops the foul balls from hitting the familias from the village who walk from thatched-roofed houses to perch on the concrete. Jokes and ribbing will fly back and forth between the rival fans, and between the players from the Coba Mayos and the visiting team—the Jaguars, from the nearby village of San Juan.

As a batter steps to the plate, you think you hear the great-tailed grackles squawking in the jungle growth. But what you're really hearing are the fans, who lift makeshift megaphones made from plastic two-liter Coke bottles cut in half. What you're really hearing are those cheering fans, calling out Maya words that carry all the way across the field, and beyond.

THE AKUMAL LIGHT POST'S DREAM

On the Akumal village ballfield, the shadow of the newly-installed light post stretches long, waiting for the cooling air of dusk, waiting for its floodlight eyes to flicker open, for the players to filter onto the crushed limestone, and for the evening game to, finally, begin.

BETWEEN INNINGS

At some tropical ball fields, a dugout is not really a dugout.

There are no steps down to it; it's built right on the ground. It might have a hard sand or gravel floor, and no bench. It might be surrounded by jungle trees and jagged chunks of limestone where—camouflaged—motionless gray and black iguanas perch. Its tin roof might be supported by angled lengths of hand-cut trees or bamboo.

But the players are thankful for what they have.

The tropical dugout—it's a place with a little shade, to shelter you from the heat of el sol in the afternoon. It's a place for teammates to linger between innings, and maybe glance at your girlfriend or wife's name, accompanied by an encouraging emoji, written in marker the back of the *Local* sign. A place where you take long a drink from a bottle of sweet mango-flavored Jarritos soda, smile, gaze up at the sky for a few minutes, and make a wish.

PART FOUR

Late In the Season

THE 102-YEAR-OLD REMEMBERS HIS FINAL GAME

Though a lot of his memories have slipped away, like sand through an hourglass, there are a few things he still recalls vividly. He remembers the ache in his arm when he threw toward home from the far left field corner as the runner tagged, his tendons tearing out by their roots. He remembers the runner sliding and the dust and the umpire—his arms stretched out, fingers touching both horizons—shouting safe! in a voice that carried for miles.

He remembers that time he decided to steal home from third base in the ninth inning, his body slowing with each step until it seemed he was trying to run through a vat of melted tar. Nearly there, he dropped down to slide, felt the rough sand peeling away the skin of his elbow and exposing the bright red layer beneath, felt the sudden burns on his calves where dirt and gravel bit into the skin hard.

He remembers sunlight and dust and years of close games. He remembers faces of friends and enemies, faces of lovers, faces growing lines and then dissolving like lozenges in warm water. Then there were the cars parked along the foul lines, black, boxy Model T cars smoothed themselves to curved cars with running boards and then became sleek and low '70s sedans and then they shrunk to small, bright economy hybrids. A grandstand was added, board by board. Then light poles stretched upward and lit the field.

There were earthquakes and floods and droughts and blizzards. And that painful trail of wars. The boys were over there in trenches on the Western Front; they marched toward Hitler, then retreated from Hanoi and drew parched lines in a desert storm. How could he forget the missiles poised and missiles dismantled, presidents and leaders rising to podiums and then slumping forward? Then there were the cries for justice and the cities burning, the glow in the sky spreading all the way to his little town, the scent of smoke tainting the air for a few days. He remembers the shrieking of decades like the sound of thousand birds on wires, and the silence between the claps of a single pair of hands.

But most of all he remembers what happened when he limped toward the bench after he tried to steal home. He was out by a long shot; he feared that before he'd even pushed off from third base. As the game ended, he knew that from then on, it'd be quiet rooms with polished walls and hushed voices and sad, patronizing smiles of relatives.

He knew the way we treat what's too old.

And he knew that the past would become a roll of gauze unraveling, something to soothe the stinging strawberry burns on the elbows.

After that last play, he hobbled back toward the bench, head down, feeling stupid for trying for home, and maybe a little sorry for himself, too. Then he glanced up and saw the children. Those three small kids—two boys and a girl, about four years old—too young to understand the game. Each of them hooked their fingers into the wires and pressed their soft cheeks to the cool diamonds of the backstop fence. Playfully climbing up the fence a foot or so, they stayed there, suspended, giggling. Their oval faces looked pure as calm pools of water, their big eyes clear as a dustless sky, and they grinned at him. As if to kiss a grandparent hello, they pursed their lips, lips bright red from eating sweet cherry candy.

At that moment, the decades of competition and pain slipped from his body and fell away like a layer of skin being shed, or one-hundred-two layers.

All the years of games, all those cheers and sighs, the championships and the last-place finishes, and what he'll remember most is those children climbing on the wires of the fence. Yes, he'll remember them most of all.

WHEN THE SEASONS CHANGE

When it's abandoned on a field for years, the sun and wind and rain will eventually bleach a baseball so that its tawny brown leather cover turns white. Even its inner strings turn to strands of frost.

When you stumble upon a ball like that, you shudder, and for a moment, in the middle of a sweltering July afternoon, the field around you covers itself with a sudden layer of winter.

WHERE THE ALL-STARS, RECENTLY CUT FROM THE TEAM, WILL GO

Where will they go, now that their reflexes and strength and speed have inexplicably evaporated from them?

Some will stalk to the cliff beyond the ball field and stare off in silence at the high cool air above the ravine.

Some will yell at the insides of their stalled cars or trucks and then lower their foreheads to the steering wheel, which feels as though it won't stop turning.

A few will go to the gym early in the morning, where they'll work and work and work for hours, trying to nurse their aching rotator cuffs or torn ligaments or ripped Achilles tendons back to life.

Others will stare and stare for hours at a baseball in their hand, studying its cracked surface as if it's some kind of crystal ball that could tell their future.

Some will go to a doctor, who places their X-rays on a lighted screen and shakes his head at their cracked bones and their cartilage, torn easily as soggy paper. Still, they'll beg him—as though he were Jesus and they were Lazarus—to heal them.

Some will slip into dreams, where they take the Major League field again, surrounded by endless tiers of bleachers and the bright, deafening sounds of fifty-thousand cheering fans.

For a few seconds each morning as they wake, some will believe they're twenty-one again, and it's the first day of tryouts. Later, they'll kneel in a church in front of an altar, bow their heads, whisper a soft prayer, and ask a question that will never be answered.

Former pitchers will stroll across a ballfield barefoot, hoping the sand circle of the mound will send its power back up through the soles of their feet again. Then they'll sit down on those fields—like six-year-old kids who just lost their first game—and cry.

Some will go to taverns, lift glasses of draft beer, and study the vague, cloudy shapes left by the foam on the sides of the glass.

Some will wish and plead and bargain and lie and lie and lie to themselves.

Others will simply throw their glove hard into a corner of the basement, lock themselves into a room and stay there for a long time, refusing to eat or sleep. They will spend hours, staring at the dim ceiling, as if expecting it to rain.

Some will think about their last at-bat in the Majors, their last pitch, their last catch, or their final throw from third base. No matter if they're at a grocery store or a party or a family reunion, they're not really there, because that final play is replaying again and again in their minds like some grainy video tape.

And a few—the wisest ones—will look into the faces of their wives or children and, amazed, see the color of their eyes as if for the first time. Blue they are, and green, and brown—like the sky, like grass, like the infield. They will reach up and touch those faces. These are the players who heal most quickly, the ones who can still stroll, alone, to a small sandlot field, limping slightly as they do, gaze out at the diamond from the top of the splintered wooden bleachers and notice how symmetrical it is. From there, they'll give the field a nod and a half-smile, it as though they're recognizing a long-lost friend.

THE OLD-TIMER MUSES ABOUT HIS
HOMETOWN FIELD

I've come to understand that in the small towns like mine, there are always three things near the center of town: a church, a cemetery, and a baseball field. These three things seem to repeat themselves: the church, where I'm careful not to break a red and purple stained-glass window with a long hit that clears the outfield fence and bounds toward it. The cemetery beside the field, where the old townspeople go—a place with gray granite tombstones and bursting flower arrangements near the brown dirt rectangles of fresh graves. And then there's the ball field itself, right there between the two.

That's where I am. That's where you'll find me. I'm Lloyd Thayer, the oldest player on the town team, the Mudhens. You might have heard of us. Or maybe not.

The younger guys call me a baseball sage, like I'm a kind of crazy philosopher or something. And if you care to ask me, I'll spew some of my famous sayings, my usual head-scratchers like: "Boys, there'll be more wins than losses. And even if we lose all the games, there'll still be more wins."

Somehow the years have passed me by, slowly, yet steadily, and as of today, I've been on this squad at least twenty-five years. Or fifty. Or more, even. Don't ask me how many, exactly, because I'll just lie about it.

You know what? When you play baseball, you never get old. And I plan to keep playing for a while. For another century, at least.

THE GRAY AND BLUE DAYS

Some days, when you stare toward it, the sky is gray, and you're the only bright spot in the afternoon.

Other days, the sky surprises itself with vividness, and you're the only grayness. It's then that you believe the words *blue sky* are the two most lovely words in the English language.

But most times, days are a combination of both: bright and gray, gray and bright, the two of them blending into a third color somewhere in between.

Be ready for it. Like a lop-sided baseball, life has a way of rolling unevenly, wobbling toward you, then away, then toward you again.

THE SEASONED BALLPLAYER TAKES THE FIELD

While other people tip their chairs back and sleep, he plays ball. When other people—like that guy in the postal truck parked at the far edge of the lot—doze during their lunch breaks, he grabs his frayed duffle bag and jogs onto the field.

Aren't you a little too old for that? some of his friends ask. They laugh at the way he always keeps baseballs in the rear window of his car, and when he turns each corner, they roll from one side to the other, thumping and thumping like leather hearts.

He just shrugs, replies: *When you're an older ballplayer, you keep playing. It's just what you do. It's what you've always done.*

Sure, these days, it's just a leisurely game of catch with your former teammates. Sure, when you bat, it's all slow-pitch—no fastballs allowed. It's cracking a few fly balls toward a wood-slat fence that, each summer, seems to pull farther and farther away. And then it's easing your taped wooden Louisville Slugger onto the grainy dirt near the plate and limping out there to pick up the baseballs, all the while imagining yourself galloping across on the field. But still, it's baseball.

He knows that when you're an older player, fielding can be an adventure. You're a few steps slower, and the ball sometimes pulls a veil over itself, doing a vanishing act in the haze of an overcast sky. It's nothing like back in your high school playing days, when you'd glide across the outfield smoothly as a steel bearing across polished glass. You believed you were aerodynamic then, a wing in flight. These days, there are no spectacular catches at the outfield wall, no heroic leaps, your body rising high into the atmosphere. At least not without consequences: torn tendons, cracked bones, ripped ligaments keep reminding you. Bruises with dark stitch marks on them keep reminding you.

During today's workout, when he does manage to make a running catch of a fly ball in the field, the old feeling enters him again—the rush of adrenaline, the sensation that nothing is out of his reach.

His buddy Manuel calls out to him, pulling him back to earth. "Okay, loco amigo," Manuel puffs, his face flushed red after an hour's workout. "Enough. My legs are turning to jelly." His pal is a little overweight, has two pre-teen kids, a steady desk job where invoices pile up like snowdrifts, and a backyard patio anchored by lounge chairs for him and his wife. "Aren't you tired yet, man?"

"Tired?" he replies, a laugh bursting from his lips. "What's tired?"

While other people tip their chairs back and sleep, he plays ball.

Today, when he finally climbs back into his car, a yellowed leaf from an overhanging tree branch flutters to the windshield and presses its palm there, just to remind him. Just to remind him. In late September, leaves will fall, and days will shift, pulling the seasons out from under you before you even realize it.

Staring past the leaf, he sees the driver in the mail truck, still slouched and dozing behind darkened glass.

He clicks the ignition and starts the car. He tells himself that he has enough time for sleeping. He has the rest of eternity for that.

THE ANCIENT ONES

Sometimes you might find a ball that's been hidden in the overgrown grass for what seems like centuries. It'll be half-submerged in the soil, as if it's been taking root. The cover is partially eaten off by the teeth of rain and snow, leaving only odd-shaped patches of leather, like continents separating during the ice age. It's a miniature earth, a world unwinding and gone awry, but still holding onto its shell.

Like a tribal elder or Zen master, it has stories to tell. If you listen closely, you'll hear it beckoning you to pick it up and honor it. So you do. At that moment, you feel its deep wisdom travel through the fragile bones of your fingers, to your wrist, and all the way to the center of your being.

VETERAN BALLPLAYER IN THE THIRD BASE BAR AND GRILL

His wounds are always on the inside—they're nothing you can see.

It always happened years ago, old Elmer will tell you—in the high school playoff or a state championship city league game. In the bar, sipping a beer, the bottle slowly beading with sweat, he will tell whoever's listening about the knee: One game, after he made a great backhanded stop at third, he pivoted, felt the earth pop out of its socket beneath him. He swears he's never turned the same since, not even to look into his wife's eyes.

He pours the fresh longneck bottle of High Life into a glass, takes a sip. A mustache of white foam tickles his upper lip for a few seconds before it fades.

Your job will be to buy Elmer another beer when he finishes this one, and then to say to him: "Go on. Tell me more."

When you do, he'll gladly tell you about the elbow: on a long throw from right field to home, he heard his elbow shattering. "The sound of glass marbles clicking together," he'll say. There was no pain at first, he'll explain, "Just the sound. That damn sound." Then, a sudden stinging, as though a million bees just landed on his arm. He shakes the arm a little now, just to remind himself, to let the memory enter the bone again.

He works his way up to the shoulder. He'll tell you how the ligaments pulled as he slid past second and tried to grab the bag with one arm. "That hug cost me," he'll say, half smiling, half grimacing. He'll tell you it made a sound inside his shoulder as if someone was tearing a thick paper grocery bag in half. He could swear everyone on the whole field heard it, but all they heard was the ump leaning close to his face and bellowing Yer out!

"Ah, it's a life," Elmer muses, shaking his head, "being an ex-ballplayer. It's a full-time job, almost."

You imagine those moments replaying their bright pain over and over in his dreams at night.

When he goes on to the next injury—a rotator cuff or tendon—you realize that your job, tonight, is not to talk, but to listen to him, to be on that field with him.

A half hour later, you begin to think that maybe everything he says is true—the world doesn't end in a sudden apocalypse, doesn't explode all at once—instead, it falls apart little by little: tendon, hamstring, wrist, heart.

Finally, he leans his rotund body toward you, motions you closer with his stubby fingers, and tells you something else, a secret.

"The mind's the worst," he confides with a raspy whisper. "Injure that, and you're injured for life." He claims it's never really been the same since he

stopped playing baseball. He'll tell you about the way, lately, his mind keeps rewinding those same scenes.

"Never the good memories when you're older," he confides. "Never the good ones. Sure, I used to think about those just after I quit. You know—the catches, the late inning homers. All that. But let me tell you something. The ones that hurt, they stay with you longest." His face is like melting wax, his features drooping as he nods at the lit Hamms beer sign behind the bar, the blue waterfall tumbling endlessly onto rocks. "Those are the ones that told you you weren't as good as you damn well thought."

All night he's saved the story about the big game, and he's ready to tell you about it now, just before closing time. "It was thirty-one years ago," he begins. "A lifetime to some. But to me, yesterday."

Elmer stands in the middle of the bar and poises his rotund body in his batting stance, the smoky air hugging him. He lifts his hands to the right side of his body, his fingers curling, knuckles whitening on an invisible baseball bat.

Taking a deep breath, he closes his eyes as if some dramatic, vivid memory from years ago is appearing behind them. "That night, during the championship game, I had my big chance," he begins. "It was the last of the ninth, the game was tied…"

You find yourself leaning forward, anticipating the ending, the moment that's stayed with him all these years. Not an injury, this time, you hope, but something good: a home run, a double, a triumphant moment that wins the game. You picture the team rushing from the dugout and clustering around him, all of them leaping and patting him on the top of his ball cap. It's not just your job just to listen anymore, to endure these stories—you want to know all about this one. You really *want* to hear it, to *be* there.

You know that he's seeing it happen again in his head, that his whole life depended on that moment. But his face goes blank a few seconds, as if his thoughts are veering off the baseline. He strolls back to the table, drains his beer, steps to the bar and eases the sweating bottle onto it as though sliding the handle of a bat into a dugout rack.

Then, without another word, he limps out of the tavern, his past like a thick layer of bandages taped gently, gently around one knee.

PART FIVE

An Elusive Kind of Light

INSTRUCTIONS FOR FIXING
A BROKEN BASEBALL BAT

It was your favorite bat, so you don't throw it in the trash barrel, but take it home instead. First, on a faded newspaper in the garage, you glue the cracked wood of the thin handle, squeezing it together gently but firmly, like something you've lost and just found, like a lover that doesn't yet understand you.

Then tape it carefully, winding it around and around with adhesive tape, the kind that might be used in hospitals or by a medic in a war. You circle it in layers so thick that not even the spinning of the earth could unwind it.

You try your best to seal the pain in, make it fuse with the wood, make it part of the bat again. Like a palm reader, the wood remembers the creases in your hands that tell of your past, your future, your lifeline. It remembers your entire childhood, and keeps those memories inside the corridors of its narrow parallel grains.

The point is, whatever it takes, you try to save a broken baseball bat, then get back into the game, and play the best you can. And maybe that's all that counts. As you step to home plate again, always tell yourself that, if you've fixed it right, then, like a broken bone—or a broken heart—it's even stronger than before.

WAITING AT THE EDGE OF THE FIELD

The young kids curl their fingers into the fence and gaze in at the field where fathers and uncles and older brothers play. Soon they'll grow up, everyone tells them; their lives will change, and before they know it, they'll turn into men and women. The steps of the tall, shadowed bleachers are always looming, and some day they will have to climb them.

But they don't think about that. Right now, they wait, patient and lonely, for a foul ball to arc over the fence. Then they'll dash—with the others—to try to retrieve it.

If they do manage to get there first and grab a ball, they'll hold it high, a trophy, like the first fish they've caught.

They won't strike it with a bat or smudge it with grass stains or dirt. Instead, they'll keep it for years, until they're much older and have all but forgotten about it. Then one morning the ball will roll from a cardboard box in the attic, and it will all rush back to them: that souvenir of a spring afternoon when they were just a kid, a memory of the small but bright world where they once lived.

ODE TO THE BASEBALLS BENEATH A SNOWBANK

In the middle of the long dark sigh of winter, there is still—somewhere ahead—spring, and baseball. We have to believe that. Those winter days, we hibernate, breathing slowly and steadily, our hearts slowed down to an almost imperceptible beat. Motionless in the cool darkness, we're pulled down by deep and heavy sleep.

But the dreams, the dreams fill our skulls with warmth. In those dreams, the gray melts away, and we run barefoot onto fields filled with a green that's bright as laughter.

And when the snow finally begins to melt in March, you might see them—a cluster of baseballs, rising steadily from the white crust. They're like ancient stones finally coming up for air, or like the crowns of babies' heads just about to be born.

THE SECRETS OF WELL-USED BASEBALL CAPS

We wear them season after season, until their red or blue or green cloth seems to fuse with our skulls, making us wonder if they know everything that we're thinking.

Sometimes, after a long season, a player pulls his or her ball cap off and peers into it, the same way a fortune teller gazes into a crystal ball.

Inside, where the sweat has evaporated, they might see concentric salty rings circling and circling themselves.

Like counting the rings on a tree, a player might be able to tell how many years they've played, and, maybe, how many more they have to look forward to.

THE TIGHTLY-WOUND BASEBALL

The tightly-wound baseball is the ball that always seems to poke a hole in the sky when you hit it. It's the ball, in Little League, that gives you your Magic Swing, sending the ball farther than you've ever hit a baseball before.

There's a logical explanation for a tight-wound, of course. Perhaps the climate was unusually hot in Haiti, or Costa Rica, and perhaps the local women in the factory were upset with their husbands or frazzled by their children, or angry at the looseness of the world. On a specific morning at one spool, a woman wound the yarn tighter than she's ever wound it before, tugging at it with each rotation until the pain subsided, and in its place appeared a symmetrical, firm sphere.

The tight-wound is the baseball that spins during your afternoon nap; sometimes it unwinds as it spins, spooling out yards and yards of blue yarn, but by the time you wake, it will have rewound itself, slipped its leather clothes back on and sealed them again, seamlessly, with close-knit stitches.

The true tight-wound can be sensed by an uneasy pitcher as he squeezes and rotates it with his hand; the true tight-wound whispers to the lines on the palm, saying *I will be gone soon.* When a pitcher senses the taut leather of a tight-wound with his fingertips, he wishes he could toss it away into the scrub brush beyond the third base line.

But for the batter, the tight-wound is prized. He wants to see it rotating toward him with that welcoming, flip-flopping smile. His eyes widen as the ball reaches the plate, wood and leather kiss for a split second, and he sends it up, up, up, high enough to land over the fenced, and into the bleachers of his dreams.

FINDING YOUR WAY HOME

No matter how lost you think you are, it's always there.

But it's not an easy place to find, and some people spend years looking for it. Some spend a lifetime.

It's often hidden in the maze of tall grass and weeds. Sometimes it's flat, and level with the earth, and it points toward the horizon. Other times, it's bent and curled around the edges, as if it's giving you a faint smile. It can be clean and bright, like it was just placed on a field last week, or it can be faded, scuffed and scarred with decades of hieroglyphic cleat marks no one can possibly read.

Sometimes, though it's only 90 feet away, it might as well be a million miles. As we take our first steps toward it, our legs seem to fill steadily with heavy hourglass sand. We begin to wonder if we'll ever get there. As we run, our footsteps make a soft gasping sound in the gravel, and we hear voices that remind us of our mother or father, urging us on, calling *You can do it! Go! Go!*

In the back of our minds are the words Out, or Safe, and we wonder which it will be. There is no in between.

No matter what, it's always there, waiting patiently to feel the touch of the sole of our foot, our outstretched fingertips as we dive for it. And when we reach it—oh, if and when we finally reach it—we exhale a relieved sigh and know exactly where we belong.

A CERTAIN SPRING THAW

There are players—especially the veteran ones—who think that the game of baseball might be some kind of fountain of youth. Though the infield is dry, it seems to quench their thirst. When they stand in the outfield, they can feel the nudge of grass as it grows right beneath their cleats.

Though they might look aged to the people around them, when they play, these older players have the sensation that the skin on their sagging faces is tightening, that their legs, their arms, their whole bodies are becoming younger, faster, lither.

If there is snow or ice anywhere near them, it always seems to be melting. After all, they'll tell you, time is a melting stream that meanders, but never stops flowing.

When they make an acrobatic over-the-shoulder catch at shortstop, they call out like joyful ten-year-olds, retrieving the laughter that's been buried somewhere deep in their childhoods.

If only for a few minutes or an hour, they tip their heads back and reach their gloves toward the sky, as if they could stir its endless blue lake, and they believe.

CYRUS: A DAY IN THE LIFE OF A GROUNDSKEEPER

So much depends on this small baseball field, Cyrus thinks, a field set between the rows of the corn field and the pale stones of the cemetery. So much depends on the way he tends the grass, watering it and watering it on the last days of summer, so that it glows green as long as it possibly can. He waters it until the grass blades reach up with thin fingers to touch the leather soles of his work boots as he walks. No matter if the people in town say he's obsessed with this field and call him weird, he knows a lot depends on the way he bends down to check that white chalk line along the third and first base lines; he knows if he wavers the slightest bit, fair becomes foul, foul fair.

This field will be ready, waiting for anyone to step onto it: the little league kids, the high school squad, the amateur team, or the older guys who just stop out for a casual game of catch or batting practice. There are no bad hops on his field—it's hard enough to catch a whirring grounder without it hitting a rut and taking a vicious jump toward the face. It's hard enough to run across the outfield for a long drive without a low spot pulling the ground out from under you, throwing you off balance.

Balance: that's a groundskeeper's credo. Balance and leveling and balance.

When he mows the field, he loves to begin mowing at the outside edge of the pitcher's mound, and then circle around and around, the way his father taught him. Each circle surrounds the one he's just mowed. Sometimes when he's finished, he climbs to the top row of the bleachers and gazes out at the nap of the grass, carved in a spiral. And he thinks *Yep, that's it, all right.* He thinks about how you start with one small circle, then make a second one, a little larger than the one before. He thinks about how, eventually, you could mow around the whole planet that way, circles around circles. All the while, almost without your knowing, the sun circles across the sky and the earth circles around the sun. It's then that—feeling suddenly a little dizzy—he realizes how tiny his life is, how humble we all should be, and how he's not much different than a single blade of grass, circled by billions.

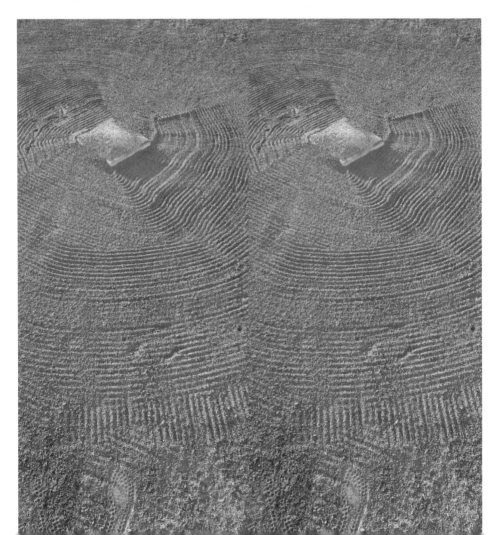

PAUSING IN THE MIDDLE OF A SMALL-TOWN FIELD

At first, you think it's an empty, lonely field. But it's not. If you stand here long enough on this day, June 21, the solstice, you'll notice a light breeze lifting its head, urging the grass blades to do a waltz with each other. Tufts of clover light pink fires and offer them to the sun. The blue sky takes a deep breath and holds it, turning itself even more blue. You gaze out at the expanse of grass, grass that extends to the wooden outfield fence, seems to pause there a moment, then stretches itself the rest of the way to the horizon.

You think it's a silent field, but it's not. Put your ear to the ground. Listen: you can hear all the way to the heartbeat at the center of the earth.

AMATEUR LEAGUE GAME WITH FIVE SPECTATORS: A BASEBALL STILL LIFE

All evening, the sounds carry as if in an empty Gothic church: each grunt and spit of batter, each gasp of footstep as a runner digs for first on a grounder, his batting helmet clunking to the hard ground behind him, each mutter after he's thrown out, the ball hitting the pocket of the first baseman's mitt with a low-pitched *pwopp*.

For some reason no one talks it up tonight, as if they're afraid of their own echoes bouncing off the paint-chipped concrete grandstand.

The 21-year-old pitcher, the bill of his cap looming over his face like a dark sky, leans in for his sign, leans so far he could tip forward into the future.

In the humid air, his nod to the catcher makes a creaking noise.

The second baseman's girlfriend—who will be married to him in the fall, and divorced from him in two years—lifts her plastic cup of lemon-lime soda just a fraction from her too-red lips and balances it there without taking a sip.

At last, the pitcher raises his arms into the stretch, tilts his head to check the runner at first, and holds there, shoulders rigid, the ball and glove poised close to his chest, holds for years, as if holding will stop the gray from creeping up his temples like vines, stop the creases from denting his cheeks, holds there until the Neanderthal umpire, his back permanently rounded, has a notion to call time out, but doesn't.

When he finally pitches the ball, a lone newspaper photographer's camera clicks, the flash bright in the corner of everyone's eyes, and decades later, the photo, curved on a dusty archive shelf, yellows.

THE MAN WHO RESCUED BASEBALLS

If you've ever walked through the long grass at the edge of a ball field, stepped on what you thought was a small mound of dirt pushed up by a mole, and looked down to see a baseball, then you'd know what he feels. He is the man who rescues baseballs.

He is the person who walks the perimeter of every ball field in town, the one who combs the field with his palm, hearing a curious litany running through his head: *Give me your tired, your poor, your huddled masses yearning to breathe free. Send these—the homeless, the tempest-tossed—to me.* The best way to find them, he'll tell you, is by bending to one knee, then looking at the field from different angles, your head tilted left or right. The best way to find them is by stepping into the scrub brush behind the backstop where nobody walks, where floating spiderwebs sometimes cling delicately to your face, or small, sharp branches lash across your cheeks.

Sometimes he finds them white and almost new, but usually he finds them weathered, tawny, like the tops of small skulls half-submerged in the soil. When he picks them up in spring, he sees the effects of sitting motionless, abandoned during the ice and cold of a long winter. They're heavy with water, and sometimes their seams are separated with a painful grimace, exposing the frantic windings of string within.

At times, he begins to think that he really doesn't find the baseballs; it's the baseballs that find him. They search him out, lift themselves toward him when they see his long legs come swinging through the spokes of grass. *You,* they seem to be whispering in their leather silence. *You.*

He's kind to each new find as he cleans it with a soft towel. He learns every stitch, learns to recognize the faces of his adopted children. When he jogs to a field, he pulls them out of the duffel bag and greets each one. He even gives them nicknames, depending on their behavior, and writes them in blue ink on their covers: *Bleacher Boy, Go-Go, Sky-Rider, OverTheFence, Above and Beyond, Escapee, Off the Wall.* A ball that hit a tree became *Tree Strikes and You're Out.* A ball that rolled to a stop on top of a sewer grate was dubbed *The Grate One.*

He has their family backgrounds down pat. He might hold a recent find close to his lips and tell it, "You're from the proud lineage of Spaldings." Or: "You're one of the Rawlings, tough and tenacious." Or: "Never forget that you belong to the royal family of Diamonds."

Then there are the others with the mixed or unknown heritage—those worn, tired baseballs that have been hit so many times that all their markings are gone, and they'd never be identified by their family names. They're often dark brown, not much different from the round stones that have pushed their way up for a breath of air in the spring. It's these baseballs he loves the best: They're the experienced ones, they're the survivors. He studies their mapped surfaces; before they were misplaced, they might have scraped against the clouds, or bounced on asphalt that left bruised scuff marks; they might have rolled all the way from New York to California.

He often thinks of those careless people who leave baseballs on a field. He often thinks of those in a hurry, those impatient people with no time or care, those who would rush to their shiny cars and leave the small things behind to die and rot. He dislikes those types, dislikes their indifference toward everything that matters.

He's not in a hurry. Even though his friends say it sounds a little weird, he could spend all afternoon searching the edges of a field just to lift a single ball, because he knows he is the one it has been waiting for. He recognizes the faces of the lost, because he is one of them.

He collects them all, cherishes them, brings them home to his young son, a boy that he hopes will, someday, be a finder of lost baseballs.

THE HOMETOWN BOYS MARK THEIR CALENDARS

Chicken wire stretches in front of the grandstands so no baseballs can flutter through. Old men, John Deere mesh caps pulled low, sit in the front row, peck and peck at the ump's calls. The 30-somethings cluster on the flatbeds of pickup trucks, cans of Bud Light sweating in their hands. Down the third base line, dressed in red or pink tank tops, the players' girlfriends languish on the hoods of their boyfriend's souped-up Chevelles or Cameros or Novas, Springsteen crooning "I'm on Fire" through a scratchy car's a.m. radio. They snap Spearmint gum on close plays. Still too young to play, kids fidget on the top row, gaze at the layer of clouds that linger over the town.

Each solid crack of the bat echoes off the welded iron grandstands, a rusty music that carries to Main Street, and you bet those fans rise to their feet and crow.

Some players claim that they'll jump into their pickups and leave this town someday, when they're ready. They mark Xs on their calendars with dulled pencil leads. Meanwhile, they wait for a slick-suited scout to walk up, tap them on the shoulder with his lightning-bolt finger.

For the time being, they come from silos and barns and expanses of alfalfa to this four-acre field, more level and close-cropped than any they've seen.

The fans know that no matter how good the pitcher, the hometown boys will hit that tomato every time. And if there wasn't a vine-covered outfield fence to stop it, the ball would roll for miles, all the way to the cornfield of their father's farms.

THE OPENING

Though you might feel as though you're trapped inside a net, it's not true. There's always a way out.

Somewhere, there's a hole in the net that leads to the sky where clouds have opened their wings. Look up: you'll find it.

PAIR OF CLEATS, LEFT ON AN EMPTY INFIELD

Life is full of mysteries, and sometimes the best we can do is ask questions. Who or where is this player, the one who left his cleats in the batter's box?

After years of playing, did he score one last run, stepping lightly on home plate, and then abandon his shoes beside it as an offering? Or did he, on his final at-bat, simply rise out of them? Was he taken up like a swirling vapor or a dust devil, lifted high, higher, higher, where he could walk, barefoot, across the bright, endless field in the sky?

THE FINDING

When a baseball is struck by an indifferent lawn mower blade, its universe is suddenly cut into pieces. Sometimes its cover is gouged with a deep scar, and other times it's torn wide open.

Sometimes its cork heart is sliced in half.

Left in the bowed grass, it bleeds beige and blue-gray yarn.

If a a lawn crew person stumbles upon it, they'll most likely throw it in the nearest trash barrel.

But a scarred ball can still dream. It dreams of a young child discovering it, picking it up, turning it over and over in his or her palm. It dreams of that child running home with it, its leather cover fluttering like a wing.

BATTER'S BOX HIEROGLYPHICS

If we were asked to interpret them, we'd ponder them for a long time, and finally say they are the markings of the first ancient humans who trudged the earth two-hundred thousand years ago.

We might speculate that they are the symbols left by the same round-shouldered hominin who placed their handprints on the walls of caves or carved petroglyphs, causing stone to come to life.

Expert anthropologists might study them, and conclude that they represent rivers and mountains, serpents and other spirit animals, the sun god, ancestral tribal members, fire, or even eternity.

We might conclude that the hieroglyphs are not translatable, that they represent a lost, undecipherable language, etched into sand with stone tools, soon to be smoothed over by the wind.

But a true ballplayer will recognize them as marks from a game that ended an hour ago—a quick-step dance of players who briefly lingered near home, or touched it with their toe, and then casually walked away.

A SONG FOR HANK AARON'S SWING
In memory of Hank Aaron, 1934-2021

Hank, your swing was so smooth, it could have been a paintbrush, sweeping broad strokes on the horizon. In '74, you stood in your tall, relaxed stance, poised on the edge of Ruth's home run record. You watched the ball roll from the pitcher's fingers, saw it rotate in the air, and waited.

As a kid, you learned your quick, last-minute swing with a broomstick, swiping at curving bottle caps pitched to you by your brother. Batting cross-handed, you were the beauty of opposites, your thin arms coiled with power. You always let your strong silence speak for you.

Once, at Milwaukee County Stadium, I watched you hit what seemed to be an infield pop-up toward the third-base line. The ball climbed the air and kept climbing, and didn't stop until, far beyond the outfield fence, it poked a hole through the glass floor of heaven.

For years since that game, I've replayed that hit in my mind: That homer was you, Hank, rising so modestly, pushing your shoulders against the heavy sky that tried to hold you down.

When you were just one swing away from The Babe's record, some idiot fans, seeing only black and white, sent you death threats.

But you knew a baseball must be set free. So you swung like you always did, and hit the ball squarely, in the place where the whorls in the wood kiss leather goodbye. The ball rose high and far for three decades, high above the shacks of Mobile where you grew up, high above the Negro leagues, the restaurants where they'd break your team's plates after you ate dinner, high above the bigots who walked off the field the moment a black man stepped onto it, and high enough to clear that wall called America.

When the ball landed in our backyards on a spring afternoon, our small sons and daughters ran over and picked it up. Not knowing it was from you, Hank, they laughed and began a game of catch, tossing the ball back and forth through the fragrant, colorless air.

THE ON-DECK CIRCLE

It feels like you've been waiting in this small circle for hours, years, your whole life. And maybe you have. But you need to understand that this circle, made with chalk dust, will eventually be circled by other circles.

Some of those circles might close in and tangle around you, making it impossible to move. A cloud of chalk dust might rise up and blow into your face, blurring your vision, leaving a bitter taste on your lips. This might not be your time: Maybe you're either too eager, or not eager enough. Or you're distracted—maybe there's a voice calling to you in the distance, someone's hand, not quite touching you, the weight of a shadow on your back, or a scarlet bird, suddenly swooping overhead.

Though you might not believe it, your time in the on-deck circle won't last long. It might sound like something a grizzled coach would mumble, but it's true: Just have patience.

Then take that first step into your future.

INHALING: ONE MOMENT IN THE OUTFIELD

That spring morning, as I stood in the outfield, waiting for my son to hit me a fly ball, I reached down, plucked some blades of grass, held them a few seconds. I let them spiral from my fingertips, studying them as if to check the direction of the wind, or to read a sacred message of some kind.

I knew I was always able to judge the wind. As a kid in little league, I could always catch the breeze in my open palm and tell if it was blowing toward right or left field, if it was stirring up a storm, or rippling the sky slightly like the surface of a calm pool.

Suddenly the thought struck me that, almost without my realizing it, the years of my life had fallen away like playing cards spilled from a table. The catches or drops didn't matter anymore. Nor did the hits or outs, the final numbers scribbled on scorecards.

What mattered was that I was there, on a field, the lips of the wind lightly kissing my face. I inhaled a deep breath of early spring air and held it, taking a few seconds to appreciate everything around me: the groomed outfield—like Adam's grass in the garden—that smelled like aromatic incense. Cumulous clouds lift from the horizon, billowing like the whipping cream on top of sundaes I savored as a kid. The distant bases on the infield, pale as hosts. And standing close to home, my dear wife and our son, the morning light angling toward them in shafts of gold. The only thing that mattered was that moment of love, that moment of exhilaration as I exhaled. And I thought to myself that it wasn't a cathedral, or a religious shrine that surrounded me, but something like it.

THE WHISPER OF OLD BASEBALL PHOTOS

They exhale the past. They freeze long-lost moments: a batting-stance pose in the yard, a blurred half-swing, a shoestring catch, a league champs grin. They're a half-opened window to your former self, a place where you once gazed up at the stars. They try to hold onto the brightness of youth, even though youth might be dulled and tarnished by time.

The photos hibernate in a drawer, stacked and sleeping inside an unsent envelope with a hand-scrawled address too faded to read.

Open the drawer. Lift the photos out and slide them across each other. Their glossy surface will sigh, and you might hear them whisper their sepia or black and white words: *Look at me. How much do you remember?*

THE HEAVEN OF BASEBALL

After Nathan, at age seven, asked "What if a game was tied forever?"
—in memory of Dale Bailey

If they made leaping catches at the fence, then they leap again and again, snagging the ball each time in the tips of their gloves. If they hit grand slams, then the bases are always loaded when they step to the plate, each pitch a high fastball they could fall in love with. If they pitched a no-hitter, their fastballs are blurs in high-speed photographs, their curves sliver the plate's corners like the edges of razor blades. If they were umpires, all close calls are fair, and no one, no one argues.

The players shrug at one another, amazed: Bruises on their knees fade and disappear, blisters on their palms smooth themselves over. The splintered bats they broke last night have healed themselves, the grains fusing together.
In the bleachers, fans scream in ecstasy with voices that never get hoarse. A crippled child stands, walks toward the railing for autographs.

After days, players in the on-deck circle gaze into the shiny surface of batting helmets, notice their faces still don't need a shave. Their skin glows without wrinkles, like in their first Little League snapshot taken in the back yard by their fathers, who never died, who still sit proudly behind home plate, cheering.

The teams could play another month, a decade, a century without rain or winter or hunger. Between each inning the players jog toward the dugout, glance at the endless lines of zeros on the scoreboard, then nod and grin at their opponents.

Finally they understand that nobody wins this one, and nobody loses. The whole world is smooth and flawless as a new baseball.

AN ELUSIVE KIND OF LIGHT

When you're an aging ballplayer, what you lose is not your old glove, that oil-softened mitt you used each season from little league to high school until its leather fused with your flesh. Even though it was left behind in a sagging box in the attic, or maybe forgotten on a dust-blown field somewhere, the glove is not what you lose.

What you lose is not that faded Honus Wagner baseball card, passed down from someone's dad, then traded from kid to kid on playgrounds. What you lose is not that valuable card, kept in a shirt pocket until your mother washed it, and the card disappeared, shred by fibrous shred, into the soapy water swirling down the basement drain.

What you lose is not that fat-barreled Babe Ruth model bat you stumbled on as you walked through the weeds at the edge of your neighborhood field. After you cracked the bat on an inside pitch, you pounded a nail into the thin handle, then circled it with masking tape, bandaging it like a broken ankle bone, and leaned it in its familiar corner in the garage. One day your parents moved to a different rental house, and then another, and piled the things from the garage into boxes, and those boxes into other boxes, and those boxes into trucks, and you never swung with that bat again. You think you've lost it, but what you lose is not that bat.

What you lose is not your Little League Champs T-shirt, a shirt that shrunk smaller and smaller each year, tightening its grip around your waist and shoulders, a T-shirt that sprung holes in front and back, holes that grew larger and larger as if the shirt were gradually eating itself alive.

What you lose is not that championship game you replay in your mind for thirty years. It's not that pitch you keep seeing, the pitch you should have hit, the baseball's seams always pink as stitch marks from a scar that won't heal. It's not that looping fly ball you should have caught, a ball that falls in front of you, sinking slowly, like a wish you didn't make, like a coin dropped just beyond your fingertips into a deep well. It's not those moments, though sometimes they circle painfully in your brain, like limping, injured dogs.

When you're an older ballplayer, what you lose is not that vacant lot where you played, a small field with a warped wooden board for a home plate and two worn spots in the grass where batters anchored their feet. What you think you lose is that small wood-slat fence at the edge of the field, and the row of pine trees, and beyond it, a field of tall grass that, as you stood there, staring, seemed to stretch across the plains and all the way across America.

What you think you lose is that field in the evening when you were seven. It was a place where fireflies rose from the deep grass and into the air, their tiny yellow lights blinking at you as you tried in vain to catch one in your cupped hand. Every few seconds, they'd light up, but always somewhere else. When you asked the man who walked by your side how fireflies can glow like that when they're only insects, he said he didn't know. It wasn't electricity, exactly, he told you, but a power we humans didn't understand, an elusive kind of light. As you walked home, he slid his arm around your shoulder and told you a story about how each tiny firefly is like the soul of a person.

That field is gone; an aluminum-sided rambler suffocates home plate. You still have memories, but they aren't what eat away at you little by little, they aren't the real things you lose. There will always be gloves and cards and T-shirts and games and fields. The real thing you lose is more important than any of those.

What you really lose is the person who took you to that field each day, the person who always walked by your side. What you really lose is that act of lifting your baseball in the stillness of late afternoon and tossing it across the blue air between you and your father. What you really lose is that game of catch, that arcing connection between your hand and his hand. For hours, the ball wove back and forth, sewing your palm, from a distance, to his. You can replace all those other things, but what you really lose is that.

Years after your father is gone, something tells you to walk at dusk from your house to an empty field at the edge of town. At the field, you pause, seeing a few blinking lights above the grass. You believe your father could be there, in one of those faint, tiny lights—speaking to you in a flickering code you can't quite understand.

So you stroll toward the center of the field, surrounded by those tiny illuminations that glow yellow for an instant, then go dark, then glow yellow again, but always in a different place. And though you know how hard it would be to catch one, you still reach out with your cupped palm. You reach out, as if you believe it would be that easy to grasp an elusive kind of light.

*   *   *   THE END   *   *   *

Credits and Acknowledgements

Several excerpts in this collection are taken from these books by Bill Meissner: HITTING INTO THE WIND (short stories), Random House Publishers, New York, SPIRITS IN THE GRASS (a novel), University of Notre Dame Press, THE SLEEPWALKER'S SON (poems, Ohio University Press), AMERICAN COMPASS (poems, University of Notre Dame Press) and THE ROAD TO COSMOS (stories, University of Notre Dame Press).

Stories and excerpts in this collection have been previously published in magazines, journals, newspapers, and other media. I'm grateful to the following publishers and publications for their permission to reprint them:

MINNESOTA MONTHLY: "An Elusive Kind of Light," "Tough Luck Ballplayer in the Diamond Bluff Tavern"

RANDOM HOUSE PUBLISHERS: "Chalk Lines" (from HITTING INTO THE WIND, a collection of short stories), "Note Left for the Widows of Over-Thirty Baseball Players," "The Heaven of Baseball," "Zen and the Art of Outfielding" (excerpts taken from a story originally entitled "The Outfielder")

THE UNIVERSITY OF NOTRE DAME PRESS: "For Those Who Choose to Hit into the Wind" (from SPIRITS IN THE GRASS, a baseball novel).

OHIO UNIVERSITY PRESS: "The Baseball Lover" (from THE SLEEP-WALKER'S SON)

AETHLON: JOURNAL OF SPORTS LITERATURE "Instruction Manual: Some Basic Skills, and One or Two Extras," "Inhaling: One Moment in the Outfield," (excerpt from "The Language of Batting Gloves") "The Old-Timer Muses About His Hometown Field" (excerpt from the short story "The Three Things, and Something Else.")

NINE, A JOURNAL OF BASEBALL HISTORY AND CULTURE: "The 102-Year-Old Player Remembers His Last Game," "The Sound of the Bat," "Instructions for Fixing A Broken Baseball Bat." Excerpt from "Tough Luck Ballplayer in the Diamond Bluff Tavern." "The Dreams of Batting Gloves" "The Heart of the Baseball" (as 'The Tightly-Wound Baseball)," "The Sound of the Bat," "The Hometown Boys Mark Their Calendars."

SPITBALL: THE LITERARY BASEBALL MAGAZINE: "Baseball Wife at the Start of the Season"

MINNEAPOLIS REVIEW OF BASEBALL: portions of "The Ex-Baseball Star Steps Out of Retirement"

Portions of "The Loneliness of the Long-Distance Outfielder" also appeared in THE MINNEAPOLIS STAR TRIBUNE SUNDAY PICTURE MAGAZINE, THE MIAMI HERALD SUNDAY PICTURE MAGAZINE, and in INDIANA REVIEW. The story was awarded a PEN/NEA Syndicated Fiction Award, chosen by Kurt Vonnegut, Jr.

INDIANA REVIEW: "The Outfielder" (original publication)

I'd like to extend my thanks to the many colleagues, friends, and former students who have supported my writing over the years, and especially to Jack Driscoll, long-time friend and writer extraordinaire.

I am grateful to the dozens of participants in The Catch and Release Baseball Club, a group of pick-up ballplayers that has taken the field during springs and summers. Mickey "Mantle" Hatten, Bill "Tater" Kaeter, Steve "King of the Diamond" Lyon and Ted "Williams" Sherarts are veteran members, and Dale Bailey (RIP) is a founding father. Author Tim O'Brien remains as our most literate participant, and Emmy-winning broadcaster Bob Costas has acted as our absentee celebrity color commentator.

Sections from some of the writings in this collection appear in appear in LIGHT AT THE EDGE OF THE FIELD by Bill Meissner. I am grateful to Stephen F. Austin University Press for permission to reprint the excerpts from the following pieces: "The Things You Lose: An Elusive Kind of Light," "Veteran Ballplayer in the Third Base Bar and Grill" (with a different title) "Inhaling: One Moment in the Outfield," (excerpt from "Circling: the Outfield Dancer") "The Old-Timer Muses about His Hometown Field" (excerpt from "What's Missing: The Three Things, and Something Else"), "Baseball Wife at the Start of the Season," and "Take a Walk Around this Abandoned Baseball Field: A Romance."

The two photos accompanying "Note Left for the Widows..." and "The Old-

Timer Muses About his Hometown Field" were taken by the lovely and talented Christine Meissner.

Thanks to her for her insightful suggestions on both the writing and the photography arrangement in this collection.

About the Author

Minnesota writer and teacher **Bill Meissner** grew up in Iowa and Wisconsin and has been a lifelong baseball enthusiast and/or player. In recent years, he's been taking photos of the unique, nostalgic settings of small-town amateur baseball fields. As his collection of photos grew, so did the idea of writing short prose pieces to accompany them. The result is this book. Meissner is the author of ten books, including three previous baseball-theme books: *Hitting into the Wind, Spirits in the Grass*, a novel, for which he won the Midwest Book Award, and *Light at the Edge of the Field*, published by Stephen F. Austin University Press in 2021. He has written articles for the *Minnesota Twins Magazine, Minnesota Monthly*, and *Baseball Cards Monthly*, for which he interviewed such baseball stars as Nolan Ryan, Kirby Puckett, Ken Griffey Jr., Paul Molitor, Dave Winfield, and Don Mattingly.

His latest book of poetry is *The Mapmaker's Dream* (Finishing Line Press). His previous poetry books include: *American Compass* (U. of Notre Dame Press), *Learning to Breathe Underwater* and *The Sleepwalker's Son* (Ohio U. Press) and *Twin Sons of Different Mirrors* (Milkweed Editions). His newest work of fiction is a novel set in the turbulent late-1960s entitled *Summer of Rain, Summer of Fire*. His chapbook of poems and short stories is *The Glass Carnival* (Paper Soul Press).

Meissner has won many awards for his fiction and poetry, including an NEA Creative Writing Fellowship, a Loft-McKnight Award for Poetry, a Loft-McKnight Award of Distinction in Fiction, a Jerome Fellowship, and a Minnesota State Arts Board Fellowship. His fiction and poetry have appeared widely in over 350 magazines during the past years, and his photographs have appeared in several magazines.

Bill's varied jobs and activities during his high school and college years have included: baseball umpire, railroad worker, circus vendor, radio DJ, and garage band guitarist. His first professional 'writing' job was a Parts Abbreviator in a warehouse—where he shortened the descriptions of various hardware items. After receiving an MFA in Creative writing from the University of Massachusetts, he has enjoyed his career as a creative writing teacher at St. Cloud State University in Minnesota.

Bill's hobbies/interests include travel (including Mexico, St. Thomas U. S. Virgin Islands, Costa Rica, and Puerto Rico), rock music, photography, pulp fiction magazines, vintage typewriters, and baseball. He enjoys being a visiting writer at various elementary schools, high schools, and colleges, and acts as an occasional writing coach.

He lives with his wife, Christine, in their home base of St. Cloud, Minnesota and plays occasionally with a pick-up group called The Catch and Release Baseball Club. Their son Nathan is a lifetime member.

His Facebook author page is https://www.facebook.com/wjmeissner

CPSIA information can be obtained
at www.ICGtesting.com
Printed in the USA
BVHW021918070322
630842BV00015B/842